Two's Company

"So who *is* going to have Jasmine?" Neil asked anxiously.

"That's just it, lad," said Henry sadly. "There's no one now. Besides us, there wasn't anyone at poor Willy's funeral. He was pretty much on his own."

"So it may well be that she'll end her days in boarding kennels," Mrs Dickens added. "Perhaps it would be kinder if she were put down. Some dogs never really get over their owners' deaths."

"She can't be put down!" cried Neil.

Titles in the Puppy Patrol series

More Puppy Patrol stories follow soon

Puppy Patrol
Two's Company

Jenny Dale

Illustrated by

Mick Reid

A Working Partners Book

MACMILLAN CHILDREN'S BOOKS

Special thanks to Vince Cross

First published 2000 by Macmillan Children's Books
a division of Macmillan Publishers Limited
25 Eccleston Place, London SW1W 9NF
Basingstoke and Oxford
www.macmillan.co.uk

Associated companies throughout the world

Created by Working Partners Limited
London W6 0QT

ISBN 0 330 48007 3

1 3 5 7 9 8 6 4 2

A CIP catalogue record for this book is available from
the British Library.

Typeset in Bookman Old Style by SX Composing DTP, Rayleigh, Essex
Printed and bound in Great Britain by Mackays of Chatham plc, Kent

Chapter One

"Ready, Jake?" Neil Parker held the gaze of his young black-and-white Border collie for just a second or two more, then curled the frisbee into the warm air of the May evening. Jake scrambled away eagerly across the exercise field that lay behind King Street Kennels. With all four feet clear of the ground he tried to snatch the flying saucer out of the sky.

But the frisbee hit him lightly on the nose and dropped into the grass. Jake shook himself and sneezed.

Eleven-year-old Neil laughed. Neil loved being with dogs. Playing with them, feeding them, looking after them when they were ill – he

1

couldn't imagine a better way of spending his time. Luckily his parents, Bob and Carole Parker, ran King Street Kennels – a boarding kennels and rescue centre near the small country town of Compton. Neil would never want to live anywhere else.

Jake picked up the frisbee and ran back to Neil for an affectionate scratch behind the ears.

"He's not much better than you at catching, is he, Neil?" shouted Emily, Neil's ten-year-old sister, as she watched Neil make a fuss of Jake.

Bob Parker was leaning on the gate next to her. "I blame the thrower, myself," he chuckled.

"Let's see how well you do then, Dad," challenged Neil. He stooped down and extracted the frisbee delicately from Jake's teeth, then quickly spun it out hard and flat towards Bob.

Jake hared off across the grass in hot pursuit.

Bob jumped to catch the frisbee as it rose up to his right, but as he stretched out his hand for it, he stumbled and lost his footing. He was a big man and he fell heavily, his back twisting as he hit the ground.

Neil started to laugh, but then stopped abruptly when he realized his dad might really be hurt.

"Dad, are you all right?" asked Emily, running over to him. For a moment there was no answer, as Bob gathered his wits. Jake licked his face.

Bob winced as he stood up. Then, as he tried to straighten up fully, he gave a grimace of pain.

"Dad, is your back OK?" asked Neil.

"I'll be fine . . . I think!" said his father rue fully, rubbing his back. "There must be some-thing wrong with that frisbee. Either that or I'm getting too old for running and jumping."

"I'm sorry," said Neil. "I shouldn't have thrown it so hard."

"Don't worry," said Bob. "I'll be fine. Now, aren't you two meant to be going over to The Grange to see Mr Bradshaw? He'll think you're not coming if you don't get a move on."

"Yeah, I guess we should be off. Come on, Em."

Neil and Emily left their dad walking stiffly back to the house, and set off for The Grange with Jake.

The best route to the old people's home was by the path that led away from King Street Kennels and traced the foot of the ridgeway towards Compton. It was a bright Friday evening, but there was no one about. Neil and

Emily let Jake run ahead. Every now and then the young Border collie would stop and turn to look at them, ears pricked and head on one side, checking to make sure they were keeping up.

It was always fun to visit Henry Bradshaw and Skye, his rough collie. It wasn't long since there'd been a no pets policy at The Grange. It had taken a lot of persuasion for Neil and his sister to convince the matron, Mrs Dickens, that neither Henry or Skye would ever be happy until they could be together full-time. But the collie's lovely nature had quickly won everyone's hearts, and over the months Mrs Dickens had mellowed. Now a couple of the other residents had their dogs with them too. Even so, Neil knew that Jake would have to be on his best behaviour or risk a severe telling-off!

They walked through the imposing gates of the big grey stone house and up to its grand entrance hall. Tom Dewhurst, the young assistant warden, strolled down the steps from the front door.

"Good evening, you two!" he greeted them. "Hello, Jake! Henry's expecting you all. He told me he's been looking forward to seeing you all day." He picked up a stick and offered it to Jake for a bout of tug-of-war.

"How's Mr Bradshaw?" asked Neil.

"He's fine," replied Tom. "You know where to find him, don't you?"

Neil and Emily nodded and made their way inside.

The Grange was like a comfortable hotel. The staircase leading to the first floor and Mr Bradshaw's room rose gracefully from the hall. Underneath Neil and Emily's feet was a new bright blue carpet.

"There you are!" a voice called from above them.

Neil and Emily looked up to see Henry Bradshaw's deep blue eyes twinkling at them from over the banister.

"I thought you'd got lost," the old man said with a smile.

Neil, Emily and Jake climbed the stairs to join Henry.

"Nice carpet, Mr B," said Emily.

"Aye, they've had it decorated again," he said as he led them along the upper corridor, waving a hand at the flowery walls. "New wallpaper too." He pulled at his white moustache. "Mind you, I thought it was all right beforehand. Now come in, come in! What have you two got to say

5

for yourselves, eh? How's young Jake shaping up?" he added, bending down towards the dog. Jake rolled over shamelessly, demanding to be tickled and fussed.

Mr Bradshaw welcomed them into his cosy room. From beside the fireplace Skye barked a welcome too and shuffled her feet. She was in the peak of condition, her amber-and-white coat shining with health. She bent her sensitive, intelligent face down to meet Jake's as he skidded over the floor towards her.

"Careful, Jake!" warned Neil. "Best behaviour, remember!"

"He'll be all right," said Henry. "If it's Mrs Dickens you're worried about, she's a changed woman as far as dogs are concerned . . ."

And before Neil and Emily could get a word in edgeways, Henry was off telling a tale about how Skye had dug up some of Matron's beloved peonies in The Grange's garden.

". . . And you know, Neil, when I told her about it, all she could say was 'These things happen!' Now a year ago, she'd have been through the roof. But having Skye around has changed things. And so did Willy Mannion's dog, Jasmine."

He suddenly dropped his head. Neil and Emily looked at each other. Even Jake and Skye, who had been busy reintroducing themselves, stopped sniffing and pawing each other and turned to watch Henry.

"Willy Mannion?" said Neil quietly.

"Yes," said Henry. "Loved animals, did Willy."

"Who is he?" asked Emily.

"He used to live here," said Henry, dabbing at his eye with the red silk handkerchief from his jacket pocket. "I'm afraid he passed away last week."

Then the old man pulled himself upright in the armchair and, smiling bravely, he said,

"But you two don't want to hear about that."

"He was your friend?" asked Emily sympathetically.

"Yes," said Henry softly. "And a very good friend he's been these last six months. We had a lot of laughs together in here, did Willy and me. I'm going to miss him. And so will Skye." He dropped a hand to his side and ruffled Skye's fur.

For a moment Neil and Emily thought Henry Bradshaw might break down and cry but he pulled himself together.

Neil stood up. "I think it's time we went home, Mr Bradshaw."

"I'm sorry to be such an old misery. You two must want to get back to the kennels." Mr Bradshaw smiled. "I'll show you out," he offered.

As Henry and Skye led the way towards the staircase, Neil noticed that the door of the room next door but one to Henry's was ajar. Jake suddenly tugged forward on the end of his lead and nosed the door wide open.

"Jake!" called Neil in embarrassment. "What do you think you're doing?"

Neil knocked politely on the door and leaned into the room, ready to apologize to whoever lived there. At first glance, the room looked empty and bare of any personal belongings. Even the bed was stripped down. But then Neil saw what had drawn Jake inside. By the bed lay a beautiful, elderly yellow Labrador, its head on its paws. The dog raised its head, and turned its sad, wet eyes towards Jake. The younger dog gave the Labrador's nose an exploratory nuzzle but was pushed gently away.

Henry stood by the door and shook his head. "That's Jasmine, Willy's dog. Goodness knows what's to become of her."

"She looks so sad," said Emily.

"She's been like this for days," said Henry. "She still won't leave poor Willy's bed. I suppose she thinks he's coming back."

Neil bent down to where Jasmine lay and stroked the smooth, creamy fur of Willy's faithful companion. She licked his hand gently, and then put her head back on her paws. As Neil straightened up, he caught sight of a harness lying on the table. He'd seen similar ones on guide dogs before.

"So Willy was blind?" he asked.

"He was," Henry Bradshaw answered. "Jasmine here was his eyes these past eleven years. And a right good team they were too."

9

No wonder Jasmine was in mourning, thought Neil. For those eleven years, she and Willy must have been inseparable.

Neil and Emily said goodbye to Jasmine and walked slowly down to the entrance hall with Henry. They were reluctant to leave Jasmine behind – she looked so sad and lonely. As they got to the front door, Mrs Dickens hurried through from the kitchens with a tray, her face flushed and her grey hair pinned up in a bun. She stopped when she saw them.

"Hello," she said. "What's with all the long faces?"

"They've just met Jasmine," said Henry.

"Oh," said Mrs Dickens thoughtfully, nodding her head. "I see."

"What's going to happen to her?" asked Emily.

"Well, to be honest," said Mrs Dickens, "we don't quite know yet, do we, Henry? I'm still waiting to hear from the Guide Dogs for the Blind Association."

Neil looked puzzled. "But I thought Jasmine belonged to Willy," he said.

"Well, not exactly," Mrs Dickens explained. "Technically she still belongs to the Association. But Jasmine's probably too old to retrain with someone else now."

"So who *is* going to have her?" Neil pressed anxiously.

"That's just it, lad," said Henry sadly. "There's no one now. Besides us, there wasn't anyone at poor Willy's funeral. He was pretty much on his own."

"So it may well be that she'll end her days in boarding kennels," Mrs Dickens added. "Though I have to say, she looks so sad, perhaps it would be kinder if she were put down. Some dogs never really get over their owners' deaths. I don't know what you think, Henry?"

The old man shook his head wearily. "I do know we'll all miss her terribly when she goes."

"She can't be put down," said Neil quickly.

"I think that Jasmine deserves a holiday at the very least," said Emily eagerly. "Would you let us take her to King Street for a few days, Mrs Dickens? We'll look after her, won't we, Neil? We promise."

Neil nodded his enthusiastic agreement. "It's a great idea, Em. We'll give her some good food, and lots of gentle exercise. And with the other dogs around her she'll soon perk up. She looks like she needs company."

Mrs Dickens frowned and looked doubtful. "I'm sure she's well fed here, Neil. Probably too well, knowing the residents. I don't know what to say. What do you think, Henry?"

Henry's blue eyes twinkled more brightly than ever. "I think it's a stroke of genius. No doubt about it. Give her a break. It's what Willy would have wanted."

"Ace!" said Neil and Emily together.

Chapter Two

Neil went to see Jasmine in her kennel at the rescue centre first thing before breakfast the next day. She struggled out of her basket to greet him with a slow wag of the tail and a couple of woofs of recognition.

"You're looking better this morning, Jas," said Neil. "Give me half an hour for breakfast, and I'll be back to take you out."

Jasmine had seemed happy to go with Neil and Emily the previous night, but she had been tired and distracted. After explanations and introductions, the Labrador had taken to life at King Street Kennels surprisingly well. Neil had fed her and bedded her down, and she hadn't complained once about the change of scenery.

13

"Are you going to be all right, old girl?" asked Neil, smoothing down her beautiful creamy coat as he talked. She licked his nose reassuringly, and shuffled back on the bed, but when he left her to go inside the house, her sad eyes followed him hauntingly.

"Neil, will you call your dad down for breakfast?" asked Carole Parker as Neil walked into the kitchen.

"Where are Emily and Sarah?" asked Neil. Sarah was his five-year-old sister.

"How could you forget?" said Carole mockingly as she laid plates out on the kitchen table. "We're off to Colshaw Town Hall this

morning for Sarah's ballet competition. Emily's helping her get ready upstairs. You could give them a shout too."

Neil went to the bottom of the stairs and called his sisters. His dad was already edging his way down, clutching at the banister.

"I feel about seventy," he grumbled.

"If your back's that bad," said Carole, "you'd better see the doctor." Neil could see that his mum was concerned.

"I really don't want to worry Alex Harvey," Bob muttered. "The only advice doctors give about bad backs is to stay in bed until it's better. And how on earth can I do that?"

"We'll cope. You know how efficient Kate and Bev are – and Neil and Emily can help out as well," reassured Carole.

Kate Paget and Bev Mitchell were King Street's kennel maids. They were a great team – energetic and hard-working too.

"Will you make it to the fête this afternoon, Dad?" asked Emily, taking her place at the breakfast table.

Bob looked puzzled.

"The *church* fête, Dad," Sarah reminded him as she breezed into the room with her pigtails swinging. "You hadn't forgotten, had you?

15

Fudge is going to win the pets' competition. You've got to be there to see that!" Fudge was Sarah's hamster. She was convinced that he was the cleverest animal in the world and was always trying to teach him new tricks.

Bob clapped a hand to his forehead in despair. "I'd completely forgotten."

Carole shook her head. "Well, you don't have to *do* anything except turn up. Kate and Bev have got it all under control."

"What's that? The fête?" said Kate as she appeared in the kitchen doorway. She brushed back her mane of blonde hair with one hand. "Yeah, no worries. It's all sorted."

"Do you need Neil and Emily to help you this morning, Kate?" asked Bob.

"I think I can manage without them," Kate smiled. "I'm sure you two are dying to take Jasmine out for a walk. She seems a lovely dog."

"She is," replied Neil. "Dad, do you think Mike Turner would have time to look at Jasmine when he comes in this morning?"

Mike Turner, the local vet, came in twice a week to check on King Street's residents, and hold a walk-in dog clinic for the general public.

"I'm sure Mike would make time," said Bob. "But I think you should find out a bit about

16

guide dogs before you take Jasmine out. She'll be used to a particular way of doing things. I'm sure there's a book around here somewhere." Bob left the breakfast table and hobbled off to the office, returning a minute or two later with a heavy reference book in his hand.

"Look at this before you go. If I remember rightly, there are standard commands all owners use with their guide dogs. If you don't use the right one, Jasmine might not know what's going on. And don't be surprised if she insists on walking to your left. It's what she's trained to do."

Neil leafed through the pages eagerly. Emily peered over his shoulder while Jake tugged at his jeans, anxious to be off.

"Don't be so impatient, Jake," Neil scolded gently. "We've got to get this right."

"Most of the commands are what you'd expect, Dad," Emily reported. "'Sit', 'Down', 'Wait', 'Come' and 'Leave' . . . That sort of thing."

"I thought I remembered it being more complicated than that," said Bob, frowning.

"There are commands like 'Forward' for moving off, and 'Over' and 'In' to bring the dog closer or further away to you," said Neil. "Nothing very unusual, though."

"OK. Well just take care, then," said Bob. He winced as he tried to sit down at the table again.

"Like you?" Neil laughed sheepishly.

The walk was no problem. Jake darted around Neil, Emily and Jasmine as they went out through the fields behind the kennels and up on to the ridgeway. Jasmine walked sedately at Neil's side, always to his left, cautiously examining this new, strange place with its expanse of lush, vivid green grass.

Neil and Emily let the Labrador briefly off the lead, to see what she would do. She lumbered a few paces, half-heartedly following the scent of a rabbit in amongst the bracken before returning to their side.

They came back an hour later to find that Mrs Atkinson had taken up residence in the kitchen, on a surprise visit from Railway Cottages, where she lived.

"Hello, Neil," said the old lady, pulling away slightly from Jake's muddy paws and brushing down her skirt. "How are you? I can see Jake's in good spirits."

"Down, Jake!" said Neil. "Keep your dirty paws to yourself."

"He's just like his grandma," sighed the old lady. "Same spirit. I could never get Betsy to restrain herself either. She was always so good with people." Mrs Atkinson reached down and tickled Jake's ears. Jake became quiet at once, nuzzling her hand affectionately.

Mrs Atkinson's Betsy had died giving birth to Jake's father, Sam. Mrs Atkinson hadn't been able to afford to look after Betsy's pups properly, and, in desperation, she had left them where she knew someone would find them. She had never had a dog since.

Fortunately, both Sam and his brother Skip had survived and ended up in good homes. Sam was very special to Neil. They had been inseparable while Neil was growing up, and Neil was devastated when Sam had died just a few months ago. The Border collie's damaged heart had failed after he'd saved his son Jake from drowning. It meant a lot to Neil that Jake was so much like his dad – strong, energetic and loving.

"You know," Mrs Atkinson said, looking up, "I could almost fancy having a dog again myself."

Carole looked at her questioningly.

"Well," she went on, "my brother Alf died a year back. He left me quite a tidy sum, you know. I could afford to keep a dog now, and I'd love the company."

Jasmine padded round the kitchen and pushed at Mrs Atkinson's leg, not wanting to be left out of the conversation.

"Mind you, he'd have to be nice and quiet. I haven't the energy to go rushing around after a puppy." Jasmine introduced herself again, this time more forcefully. "Hello!" said Mrs Atkinson to the Labrador. "You're a beautiful dog, aren't you?"

Jasmine turned her doleful eyes on Mrs Atkinson. The old lady met her gaze and stroked her smooth nose.

Neil suddenly had an idea. "Meet Jasmine," he said. "A dog like her would be perfect for you, I reckon. And she's looking for a new home."

Mrs Atkinson looked doubtful. "I don't know about that," she said with regret in her voice. "I'm probably too old to look after a dog properly. It might be too much for me to handle now—"

"Not a dog of Jasmine's age," interrupted Neil. "She's very respectable now." And he and Emily told her how Jasmine had come to stay with them.

"Hmm, very interesting," said Mrs Atkinson,

looking fondly at the dog. "I'm sure you'll find a good home for her," she added, though Neil was convinced she sounded uncertain.

"I hope so," he said, smiling.

Carole looked at her watch. "Now, I don't want to hurry you Mrs A," she said, "but I've got to dash into Colshaw with Sarah so that she can be a fairy at eleven-thirty. And Neil and Emily have got to take Jasmine to the vet, haven't you?"

"Hello, you two!" said Mike Turner as Neil and Emily led Jasmine into the converted old rescue centre where the vet held his clinic. "How's tricks? So this is the wonderful Jasmine. Bev's been telling me all about her!"

Neil watched as the vet ran an experienced eye over the elderly Labrador. "Looks healthy enough, for starters, Neil. Nice shine on that coat! She's obviously been well-cared for. Walk her round for me a moment, will you?"

Neil and Jasmine took a turn round the room.

"Hmm, she seems to move reasonably well, considering her age. What is she, about thirteen?"

"That's what Mrs Dickens said," answered Neil.

"OK, let's put your dog knowledge to the test, Neil. What should I be looking for in an old Labrador like Jasmine?"

"Arthritis?" suggested Neil.

"Well done! It's quite common in Labs as they get older. So it's good that Jasmine's moving quite freely." Mike bent down and stroked her. "Let's have you up here, old girl," he said, coaxing her up on to the table.

Emily helped her up, and the vet gave her a thorough examination.

"What do you reckon?" asked Neil.

"She's in great shape," he announced. "Her breathing's good too. She's a lovely dog but she's probably a bit old to go back to work now. Her reactions won't be what they were. She'd still make someone a smashing pet, though."

Just then, Bev slipped into the room and said something to Mike that Neil didn't catch. The vet raised his eyebrows.

"Perhaps you could take Jasmine off to the kennels for a rest, Bev?" he suggested. "It sounds like I've got a patient Neil and Emily might find interesting."

"Why's that?" asked Neil curiously.

"Coincidentally, it's another guide dog. I don't think I've examined one in the last year, and now there's two in a row. Strange!"

Bev led Jasmine away, and showed a family group into the clinic.

"Come in, Mrs Elliott. Come in, all of you," said Mike with a welcoming smile.

The woman who entered the room was smartly dressed and Neil thought she looked rather posh. With her were two children and a lively, lean young Labrador, carrying much less weight than Jasmine. Neil recognized the boy as Tim Elliott who'd recently joined his friend Chris Wilson's class at Meadowbank School in Compton. He was chunkily built with cropped fair hair and a very pale complexion.

The girl was older. She was slightly built, with very short dark hair, almost like a boy's. She was barely taller than her brother, but there was something challenging and confident about her despite her size, Neil thought. She was the one holding the Labrador too, on the end of a familiar short, framed lead.

"What can I do for you folks?" Mike asked.

Mrs Elliott cast a doubtful eye over Neil and Emily.

"This is Neil Parker, and his sister Emily," said Mike reassuringly. "They live here at the kennels – and they love dogs. What's this one's name?"

The dog held herself alertly and seemed to be glowing with health. Its coat was darker than Jasmine's, a rich golden colour.

The girl answered, "Chloe," in a cool, confident voice.

"OK, and what seems to be the problem with Chloe?" asked Mike.

"She's been sick, Mr Turner," said Mrs Elliott. "It's such a nuisance." She began a long and detailed description of a recent occasion when Chloe had been sick.

Mrs Elliott doesn't seem to like her dog very much, Neil thought to himself. There was

24

something about the way she spoke about the Labrador that seemed all wrong for this beautiful, calmly behaved dog. Neil tried smiling at Tim, but he scowled at his feet and gave no sign of recognition. The girl was tapping her foot, waiting for her mother to finish.

"Well, let's take a look at her, then," said Mike. He examined Chloe thoroughly. She was every bit as good on the table as Jasmine had been.

"Chloe's got a lovely temperament, that's for sure," the vet said. The girl smiled, almost triumphantly. "Has she been feeding well?" Mike Turner added.

"No problems at all," said the girl before her mother could get a word in. "It's stress, if you ask me."

"Oh?" said Mike, interested. "And what makes you say that?"

"You'd only have to live in our house for five minutes to know," the girl muttered under her breath.

"Charlie!" Her mother looked flustered. "If there's any stress, it's because of the way you behave. Don't listen to her, Mr Turner. She doesn't know what she's talking about."

"Don't know what I'm talking about? Don't

know?" Charlie was nearly shouting. "Whose dog is she? Who spends time with her? Who's the one who loves her? I always knew this was a complete waste of time. Come, Chloe!"

The Labrador rose and jumped down to Charlie before Mike could lay a restraining hand on her rump. Charlie turned and urged Chloe forward. She stomped her way through the door and out of the clinic.

Her mother blushed a deep shade of red and seemed to be about to say something to Mike. Then, obviously on the point of tears, she rushed after her daughter, mumbling an embarrassed apology. Tim shrugged his shoulders and, without raising his eyes, trailed off in their wake, leaving Neil, Emily and Mike looking at each other in astonishment.

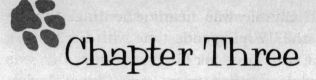

Chapter Three

For the first time in a few years, it wasn't raining on the day of the Compton church fête. Everyone was enjoying themselves on the large vicarage lawn.

Having worked all morning to set up the King Street Kennels stall, Kate and Bev had escaped to the refreshments tent, leaving Neil and Emily in charge, with Jake and Jasmine for company. Emily loved selling things to people. There were King Street Kennels sweatshirts, mugs and bookmarks and, as she told anyone passing within earshot, it was all for a very good cause.

Neil's friend, Chris Wilson, appeared at the stall in the middle of the afternoon. Jake scurried round his feet and nibbled at the laces

27

of his trainers, while Jasmine lay in the shade of the stall, keeping cool.

"Hi, Chris! You look lost," said Neil.

"Saturday afternoons are for playing football!" laughed Chris.

"Buy a mug for your mum," suggested Emily.

Chris peered at the articles for sale, looking bored.

"Hey, is there a new kid in your class? Tim Elliott?" Neil asked.

"Yeah. He's all right. Supports Everton, though!" said Chris with a grimace.

"We ran into him this morning," continued Neil. "He didn't seem very all right then. Has he ever mentioned Chloe?"

"Who's Chloe? His sister?" said Chris, casually inspecting a sweatshirt.

"No, his sister's called Charlie," Neil replied. "Chloe's her guide dog."

"Oh right," said Chris. "I'd better go. My mum's picking me up in twenty minutes, and I'm going to win a coconut if it's the last thing I do!"

"Are the Elliotts here then?" Neil shouted at Chris's retreating back.

"Yeah," Chris shouted back, waving a hand airily around the field. "They're somewhere around. And the dog."

"It's quite a coincidence, isn't it?" said Neil, stroking Jasmine as the old dog staggered to her feet for a gentle stroll around the stall.

"What is?" said Emily, counting change.

"The Guide Dogs for the Blind stall being almost next door to us. Hadn't you noticed?"

"Are they?" asked Emily. "I've been too busy selling things. Hello, Mr Hamley. Buy a T-shirt! Please!"

The headmaster of their school walked on with a cheery wave, pleading poverty.

"When Kate and Bev get back we ought to go over and introduce ourselves," said Emily. "Perhaps the Guide Dog people will tell us what they've got in mind for Jasmine. I'm desperate to know."

"Me too, but it might be bad news," said Neil, suddenly worried. "They might want to send her away to a kennels. I can't help thinking that we could find her a really good home, though. Jasmine and Mrs Atkinson are perfect for each other."

"Are you sure she should have another dog? After all, she couldn't look after Betsy's pups properly – Sam and Skip had to be adopted." Emily reminded him.

"Yes, but she made sure someone would look

29

after them – and you've seen how much she loves dogs," Neil said. "Mrs Atkinson's definitely ready for another dog now. She's got enough money and she'd love the company."

Just then Kate and Bev reappeared, with large chocolate ice creams. Jake jumped up at Kate and a melting spatter of chocolate landed on his nose.

"I've just seen your dad," she said, laughing at the young Border collie. "He's not very happy, is he?"

Neil frowned. "I still feel guilty about him getting injured," he said.

"He'll be OK," answered Kate.

Kate and Bev took over the stall and Neil and Emily wandered over to the Guide Dogs for the Blind stall. Jake ran in front of them and sniffed curiously at the pictures of dogs that decorated it. Jasmine stayed close to Neil's side.

"Well, hi there! You're a bit on the small side for a guide dog, I'm afraid!" a friendly voice said to Jake.

Standing behind the stall was a woman in her mid-twenties. She was grinning broadly. The dark fringe of her pageboy haircut framed a round face. The pictures surrounding her were of guide dogs and their blind human companions. There were golden and chocolate Labradors crossing roads and passing beside pneumatic drills, and German shepherds threading their way through revolving doors and up staircases: dogs providing sight for humans.

"My name's Syd," said the woman. "I work at the Association's regional centre in Bolton. It's where we train guide dogs and their new owners. How can I help?—" She stopped suddenly as she caught sight of Jasmine. "Well now, I know *you*, don't I? What are you doing here?" she said in surprise.

Jasmine wagged her tail energetically and, with jaws wide open and lolling tongue, she panted a greeting.

"This is Willy Mannion's dog, isn't it?" asked Syd. She came round from behind the stall and fondled Jasmine's neck affectionately. "Now, remind me," she said softly. "What's your name again? Janice. . . ? Jocelyn. . . ?"

"Jasmine," corrected Neil.

"Of course," said Syd. "I don't always remember the names but I never forget the dogs and their owners. So where's Willy?"

Neil began to explain about Willy's death, and why Jasmine was with them. Syd looked sad for a moment, then cuddled the Labrador.

"Poor old Jasmine," she said. "How's she coping?"

As Neil and Emily looked at each other Jasmine turned to lick Neil's hand. "Not very well really, but she's perked up a lot since she's been with us," Neil said.

"Well, it's very sad about Willy, but it's very kind of you to look after her," said Syd. Then, suddenly, she seemed to put two and two together. "But of course! You're from King Street, aren't you? I've heard so much about you."

"Actually," said Neil, "we wanted to talk to you. You see, we're worried about Jasmine's future—"

Just then a crowd of people began to drift by noisily. A few of them started to show interest in the stall, picking up leaflets and studying the pictures.

"Look, folks," said Syd, "I'd like to talk some more, but it seems as if we're getting busy. Do you want to come back in a bit, when the rush has died down?"

"Sure," said Neil. "We'll be there."

They left Syd chatting to a stream of curious customers and wandered aimlessly between the stalls.

"That was amazing," said Neil. "I can't believe Syd recognized Jasmine."

"Well, think about it," replied Emily. "We'd recognize a lot of the dogs that have passed through King Street, wouldn't we?"

Neil nodded in agreement. "Look who's heading our way!" he said.

About twenty metres across the grass and steering a straight course for them, were Charlie Elliott and Chloe, with a sulky-looking Tim trailing behind.

"Let's say hello," said Emily.

"You bet," replied Neil. "I want to know a bit more about Chloe. Mike never even had the chance to find out if there was anything wrong with her."

In the event, Jasmine took matters out of their hands. She went forward to meet Chloe, nuzzling and sniffing at her. Blocked by Jasmine, the Elliotts came to a halt.

"Hi there!" said Neil. "Do you remember us? I'm Neil and this is Emily. We were at King Street Kennels earlier when you brought Chloe in."

"Yes, I remember," Charlie answered in an off-hand way.

"I'm in the same year as Tim at Meadowbank," said Neil.

"Hard luck," said Charlie. Tim just grunted and scowled. Neil noticed that he was staring at Jasmine.

"Chloe's lovely," Neil went on, taking a deep breath and trying very hard not to be put off.

The girl softened slightly and said, "She's the best, aren't you, Chloe?" She reached down to caress the young Labrador's smooth neck.

"And is she really all right, like you said?" asked Neil. "Her stomach, I mean."

"Oh, that stuff with the vet this morning?"

Charlie sounded scornful. "It's just my mum being difficult. Chloe's not hers, and she doesn't understand her. Sure, Chloe was sick once, but it was no big deal. She's absolutely fine – if you know anything about dogs you'll be able to see that for yourself!"

She reached over and gently felt Jasmine's head and neck. "So you've got a Labrador too," she said, surprised. "What's her name?"

"She's called Jasmine," Emily replied. "Only she's not ours. We're just looking after her for a while." Tim gave Jasmine another hard stare and Charlie started with surprise.

"We know a Lab called Jasmine," she said. "But she belonged to a man called Willy Mannion. He lived in the same old people's home as my grandad."

Neil groaned inwardly and, for the second time that day, he and Emily had to explain how Jasmine had come to be with them.

"Mum went to the funeral with Grandad," said Charlie quietly. "She said it was really sad that Willy had no relatives." She dropped to her knees and cupped Jasmine's face in her hands. "You're going to miss Willy terribly, aren't you, Jasmine? I've only been with Chloe a couple of months – since my sixteenth birthday – and

we'd already be desperate without each other."
As if in answer, Chloe shouldered her way in to lick Charlie's nose, so that the girl was kneeling with an arm round each Labrador. The two dogs could have been mother and daughter.

As Charlie spoke, Tim turned away with a scowl.

"We're really worried about what's going to happen to Jasmine," said Emily.

"Have you met Syd from the Guide Dogs for the Blind Association?" asked Charlie, standing up again.

"Just now," replied Neil. "I was amazed that she recognized Jasmine."

"Oh yeah, she knows most of the guide dogs for miles around. We were just on our way to see her. Do you want to tag along?"

"Sure," said Neil. "We'd already arranged to go back and talk to her."

With a command of "Forward" and then "Straight on" to Chloe, they all moved across the grass towards the Guide Dogs for the Blind stall. Jake tore ahead of them and Tim trailed along at the back, his head down.

"Wow, it's great to see you again, Charlie!" said Syd, grinning. "Chloe looks fantastic. How's it going?"

"So-so," said Charlie in reply. Syd looked disappointed and concerned. "It's just Mum," the younger girl sighed.

"Well, we knew it'd be difficult, didn't we?" said Syd. She turned to Neil and Emily. "It's often hard for relatives to adjust when someone gets a guide dog for the first time. We try to make sure the whole family can cope beforehand, but there's only so much we can do."

"I didn't think it'd be this hard," Charlie moaned. "Chloe was sick once. It's nothing really, but Mum panics so quickly. I don't know what to do with her. We keep having rows."

"But she must be able to see what a great dog Chloe is," said Neil.

"You would have thought so – but things are difficult at the moment," said Charlie, scowling. He was standing a few feet away, watching the coconut shy. "I think Mum's a bit lonely. We've only been in Compton three months, you see. I don't think she found the move very easy."

"Do you want me to come and have a word later on? I've got time before I go back home," offered Syd.

"Oh, would you, Syd? That'd be brilliant!" Charlie said gratefully. "Now, come on, let's forget about me. Tell us what's going to happen with Jasmine? Will you let her stay with Neil and Emily?" she asked eagerly.

"I'm afraid I haven't heard anything about it at all, and the decision wouldn't be mine anyway," said Syd. "What would *you* like to happen, Neil?"

Without actually mentioning Mrs Atkinson, Neil explained that he thought he might have found a possible home for Jasmine.

"The Association wouldn't have Jasmine put down, would they?" asked Charlie.

Syd shook her head. "Not unless she's ill – but she is quite old, and Labs are prone to arthritis."

"It won't come to that," said Neil, putting on a bold front. "Jasmine deserves a good home – just like Chloe. Considering you've been together just a couple of months," he said to Charlie, quickly changing the subject, "the bond between you and Chloe is incredible."

"Thank you," said Charlie quietly. "I think we're lucky to have each other."

"You do realize, of course," Syd said to Neil and Emily, "that you're in the presence of a genius!"

From the corner of his eye, Neil saw Tim

shoot Syd another of his black looks.

"Oh, shut up, Syd," said Charlie, embarrassed.

"This young woman's only going to Oxford University to study Maths in October – *two years early*," Syd continued.

"Are you?" said Neil.

"Yeah," laughed Charlie.

"What's the secret?" asked Emily.

"I haven't a clue," said Charlie, looking genuinely mystified. "I've just always been very good at it."

Suddenly Tim boiled over and, for the first time, Neil and Emily heard his voice. It quivered with anger. "Me, me, me! Charlie this and Charlie that. Why does everything in our family always have to revolve around you? I hate you and I hate living here, and I've had enough! I'm going!" He turned on his heel and half-stomped, half-ran across the field.

Neil was shocked. "What was all that about?" he asked.

Chapter Four

For a moment Charlie and Syd were silent, unsure what to do.

"Don't worry," said Syd gently. "He'll be OK. Things must be difficult for Tim at the moment. Look, the fête's winding down and it doesn't look as though I'm going to be exactly overwhelmed with business now. Let's go and have an ice cream and see if Tim comes back."

They sat at a table outside the refreshments tent, and watched as the other stallholders began to dismantle furniture and pack away unsold goods. Neil shot a look towards the King Street Kennels stand where Kate and Bev were packing up. It looked like they were nearly finished.

Chloe and Jasmine lay panting in the heat, nuzzling each other affectionately. "I've got a feeling those two are related, you know," mused Syd, wiping stray ice cream from her mouth.

"How's that?" said Neil.

"Well, most of our dogs come from the breeding centre at Tollgate, near Warwick," Syd went on, "and I'm fairly sure that Chloe's mum was the granddaughter of Jasmine's mum."

"So that makes her Jasmine's great-granddaughter then?" asked Emily.

"No, a great-aunt," said Charlie. ". . . I think!"

"That's amazing!" said Neil. "No wonder they get on so well."

"Tell you what," said Syd. "Charlie and I had agreed she'd come over to Bolton one Saturday when I was free, just for fun. We could do it next week, and you two could come along as well if you like. Then you can see what we get up to. You never know, it might inspire you . . ."

"Inspire us to what?" asked Neil.

"Well," said Syd, her eyes twinkling, "you might get the urge to do some fund-raising. We can always do with the cash."

"We could organize a collection!" said Emily enthusiastically. "Or a car boot sale!"

"Good idea!" said Syd. "Though sponsored

events sometimes rake in a bit more."

"What about a sponsored walk?" Neil suggested. "For people *and* their dogs. I bet there are loads of people in Compton who'd be up for that."

"Now that sounds like a fantastic idea!" Syd leaned forward, her head on her chin. "And I'll tell you something. My boss, Martin Harrison, might well be the one with the say-so on Jasmine's future. Let's assume he hasn't got everything sorted yet. If you've got a suggestion as to where she might be placed *and* you're raising money for the Association, he's certainly going to listen to you, isn't he?"

Charlie smiled for the first time in a while. "Good thinking, Syd," she said.

That evening, as the Parkers relaxed in the living room at King Street, Neil and Emily told their mum and dad about their idea for a sponsored walk in aid of the Guide Dogs for the Blind Association.

"It looks like everyone's so booked up, there's only one day it can be," said Neil. "Saturday, June the fourteenth."

Bob Parker was lying flat on the floor trying to get his back comfortable, while Jake, who thought this was great fun, licked his face and generally made a nuisance of himself. Bob pulled himself into a sitting position. "Sounds like a great idea," he said. "But are you sure you've thought it through? Something as big as this has to be organized very carefully, and if it's got to be on June the fourteenth, you've only left yourselves three weeks to get everything together."

Carole looked thoughtful. "Well," she said, "since you're injured and can't be Mr Action Man this week, maybe you'd be able to find more time than usual to help Neil and Emily set things up."

"I'm not exactly helpless, you know," said Bob.

"Could me and Fudge do the walk?" asked Sarah. The hamster peeped out between her hands to stare inquisitively at the rest of the family.

"Sure," said Neil encouragingly. "As long as you're with a dog as well. That's the important thing."

"Go on, Dad," pleaded Emily.

"Well," said Bob, ruffling Jake's glossy black-and-white fur, "I suppose for starters I could help you sort out the route, and put the police in the picture." His eyes brightened. "It'd be good if we could use the grounds of Padsham Castle, wouldn't it? And we're going to have to work hard to persuade everyone to take part."

"Ace! I can't wait!" said Neil. "Come on, Em, you're good at lists. We need to think of as many people as possible, and start writing letters now."

"And we can put posters up round Compton," said Emily eagerly. "This is going to be the best!"

As Mrs Elliott drove them all to Bolton the following Saturday, Neil and Emily brought

Charlie up to date on developments, while Chloe dozed behind them in the back of the Elliotts' battered old estate car. There hadn't been room to bring Jasmine as well, and Tim had decided he'd rather stay at home.

Every spare minute of the last week had been spent on the phone and writing letters. Everyone at Meadowbank School had been told about the walk, and they had trawled through the Kennels database in search of yet more people who would be willing and fit enough to spend a whole day walking with their dog.

"How's Chloe been this week?" Neil asked Charlie.

"No problems at all," she answered from the front seat. "She's definitely over it—"

"She still looks a bit peaky to me," interrupted Mrs Elliott.

"I'd know if anything was really wrong, Mum," replied Charlie patiently. "She's got tons of energy, and she's been right on the ball all week."

"She looks fine to me, Mrs Elliott," said Neil, stroking the Labrador's golden fur through the grille behind him. Chloe pushed her nose against his hand and wagged her tail happily.

"Look, are you going to manage without me

today, Charlie?" said Mrs Elliott suddenly as they left Compton. "You're still getting used to Chloe, you know, and I don't *have* to go round the shops."

"I think it's more of a question of you getting used to me being independent," said Charlie crossly. "I trust Chloe. Can't you see how good we are together? And think of the money that's gone into training her. Twenty-five thousand pounds per dog! The GDBA wouldn't do that if it didn't work, would they?"

Mrs Elliott didn't reply. There was an uncomfortable silence.

"We've sorted out a great route for the walk," said Neil eventually to Charlie. "It's more or less a circle. Mrs Dickens is going to let us start and finish at The Grange. From there we can go all the way to King Street on the bridleways."

"And from home we'll go right up on to the ridgeway, before cutting back through the grounds of Padsham Castle," picked up Emily. "Then we'll make our way round to Colshaw, and finally back through the far side of Old Mill Farm to The Grange. What do you reckon?"

"I'll have to take your word for it," laughed Charlie. "I'm still getting used to where everything is round here. How far do you think the walk is?"

"Well, it looks like about twelve and a half miles," said Neil.

"And we've worked out five stopping points where dogs – and walkers – can have a drink," said Emily. "If some people can't manage the whole walk, they can wait at one of the stopping points for a lift to the finish."

"Well that doesn't leave me much to do then," sighed Charlie.

Neil sensed her disappointment. "You're kidding! There's tons. We've really got to get our act together with publicity and sponsorship. Oh, and Em and I have had a great idea. How do you fancy going on local radio?"

"Whatever!" said Charlie jokingly. "Breakfast television too, if you like."

"She doesn't think we're serious," said Neil, smiling.

"We are, you know!" Emily laughed. "Wait and see! And if Tim wants to help there's plenty for him to do too."

Charlie was silent.

"How *is* Tim?" prompted Neil.

There was another pause before Charlie answered, and for a moment Neil was worried she might be annoyed with him for asking.

"He's not too happy at the moment," she said eventually. "I suppose a lot of it's about Cosmo."

"Who's Cosmo?" asked Neil.

"He was our dog, an Old English sheepdog. Well, *Tim's* dog, to be more accurate. When we came to Compton and I got Chloe, we were a bit short of money and space."

Neil saw Sylvia Elliott shoot an embarrassed glance at Charlie in the driving mirror.

"Anyway, Cosmo had to go, and Tim was devastated," Charlie continued.

"You didn't have him put down?" asked Neil, appalled at the thought.

"Of course not! But he's gone to live with my aunt in Preston, and Tim's never been the same since—"

"Oh, come on, Charlie," interrupted Mrs Elliott. Her tone was one of annoyance but she looked uneasy. "You're exaggerating. And anyway, we didn't have a choice."

"I know we didn't, but it's true, Mum. You know it is. He always seems so angry now," Charlie added.

"I bet it'd help if we tried to get him involved in the walk," Emily suggested.

"Maybe." Charlie didn't sound too hopeful.

"Well, here we are at last!" said Mrs Elliott as the car swung into a grand driveway. Chloe stirred in the back and barked a loud greeting.

They drove through a small park and stopped in front of a jumble of buildings. An alert retriever loped past them on a path with a nervous-looking blind owner. Beside the pair walked a sighted person, offering encouragement.

Even before Mrs Elliott had parked the car, Syd emerged from the main building and waved. "You found us all right, then?" she shouted. "Fantastic! Come in and have a cup of tea."

For the rest of the afternoon, while Sylvia Elliott went off shopping in Bolton, Neil and Emily met some of the cleverest and most dedicated dogs they had ever seen.

"This is Brandy," said Syd as she showed them round the beautifully designed kennels. "She's fourteen months old, and just two months into her training with us. Before she came here, she was with one of our best puppy-walkers in Leamington Spa."

The immaculately groomed Labrador's coat was a rich chocolate-brown. She kept perfectly still and poised as Neil stroked her.

"What's a puppy-walker?" laughed Emily. "Or is that a daft question?"

"No," replied Charlie. "It's just someone from an ordinary family who takes one of the puppies from breeding and spends nine months or so doing the basic obedience training."

"Yes," Syd added. "We couldn't do without them. They make sure the puppies go out as much as possible so that they can cope with being near traffic or getting round obstacles. Later on, if Brandy does well, she'll be ready to be matched with an owner."

Chloe and Brandy stood shoulder to shoulder, completely relaxed in each other's company, as if they were old friends.

"How do you match the dogs with the owners?" asked Neil, curious about this whole new world of dogs.

"Some owners have preferences," Syd explained. "Older people might not want an animal that's too lively, and different people walk at different speeds. So we try to find everyone a dog that suits them. Labradors are the most popular breed, but we have a lot of retrievers and Labrador-retriever crosses too. Perhaps ten per cent are German shepherds, and very occasionally there are other breeds."

Back inside the main building they found the corridor almost filled by a big man with a friendly grin.

"Martin, these are the friends of Charlie I told you about," said Syd. "Neil and Emily, this is my boss, Martin Harrison."

"Hi, folks! Good to see you again, Charlie," said Martin warmly. "So, come on, Neil and Emily! Tell me about this rescue centre of yours!"

They stopped and chatted for a few minutes about King Street Kennels and about Charlie's progress with Chloe. After a while, Emily couldn't contain herself.

"Mr Harrison?" she said.

"Call me Martin. Everyone else does."

"Martin, you know about Jasmine?" Emily continued.

"Willy Mannion's dog?" Martin asked with a grin. "Yes, Syd's told me you've taken her in."

"Will she be able to stay in Compton, if we find her a home?" Emily asked anxiously.

Martin Harrison looked directly at her. "Well, to be honest I've just managed to find her a place in a kennels in Manchester."

Emily's face fell.

"But we haven't confirmed it yet," he

continued. "Syd told me you two have got your heart set on Jasmine staying in Compton – and a possible home for her in mind. If you really can come up with a suitable alternative we'll definitely consider it."

"Just give us a couple of weeks to work on it," pleaded Neil.

Martin's eyes crinkled into a smile. "That seems fair enough to me," he said.

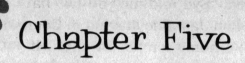

Chapter Five

"Come on, Jasmine! Keep up!" Neil bent down to encourage the Labrador. "She's getting fitter, you know," he said to Emily. "I'm sure she's lost a bit of weight in the past week." Jake raced ahead of them and sprang over a low stile as they set off towards Old Mill Farm, which bordered King Street Kennels.

It was Sunday afternoon, and Neil and Emily had decided to check out the path that led through Richard and Jane Hammonds' farm to The Grange. It was an essential part of the sponsored walk, and, as Bob had pointed out, they'd never actually used it before.

The path soon widened into an old road with high tangled hedges on both sides. Just when they thought they were nearing the farm, the path narrowed again and nettles began to grow in from the sides, forcing them to walk in single file. Then Neil came to a dead stop. Jake barked in surprise at the sudden halt.

"Hey, this is a bit of a problem, isn't it?" said Neil, wiping his brow.

"I didn't expect that!" said Emily. "Yuck, what a pong!"

In front of them the path was overgrown with nettles. Worse than that, it was completely blocked by a pile of rubble and old machinery. Jake wandered up to it and sniffed the air, while Jasmine stood obediently to Neil's left, waiting for his next move.

"What are we going to do?" said Emily. "If we can't get through this way, the whole walk will have to take a massive detour. The only other route back to The Grange is the main road through Compton."

"Mr Hammond will just have to shift the rubbish. We're on a public footpath. He's not allowed to block it!" Neil asserted. "Let's go and ask him to sort it out."

Emily thought for a moment. "No, let's go

back home and talk to Dad first. We need to tackle this properly."

"Yeah, you're probably right. Charlie and Tim are due round soon anyway."

They arrived back at King Street Kennels to find their dad attempting to help Kate with the evening rounds. Neil could see he was still in pain as he crouched down stiffly to pet an overexcited Jake. When Neil told him the news, Bob stroked his beard thoughtfully.

"That's a bit strange. Richard Hammond ought to know better. I'm sure he wouldn't want to spoil the walk, but he's a very busy man. I doubt he'll be able to move it in time."

"But the walk will be ruined!" Emily cried.

"And what he's doing is against the law," added Neil.

"Well I suppose you could try talking to him, Neil. But I don't think you should get your hopes up," said Bob.

"Perhaps taking Charlie and Chloe along would make the point. They should be here any minute – we've got to talk about plans for the walk," said Neil.

"Good idea," laughed Bob. "If anyone can persuade him, Charlie can!"

Just then Sylvia Elliott's car turned into the drive. Charlie and Chloe piled out, followed by a reluctant Tim, and Mrs Elliott waved and drove off. Tim took a football outside to practise against a wall, while the others settled themselves in the living room to talk. Chloe lay down loyally by Charlie's feet, and Jasmine lay next to her, obviously enjoying the younger dog's company.

Neil and Emily told Charlie about the problem with the path on Richard Hammond's land.

"Right," she said. "We'll go and tackle him when we've been through everything else on our list. What's first, Emily?"

They went through all the possible walkers, ticking off people who'd agreed to take part and been given sponsor forms, and deciding who would target which of the remaining names on the hit list.

"We've lined up Mrs Atkinson to walk with Jasmine," said Neil. "We told her that we didn't think Jas would manage more than one or two stages, and she actually offered to go with her. They're going to come to the start to see everyone off, and then Mum will give her a lift to King Street so that they can walk from there to Padsham Castle."

"You really are doing your best to pair those two off, aren't you?" laughed Charlie.

"Well, I reckon once Mrs A's got to know Jas a bit better she won't be able to resist!" said Neil. "Oh, and by the way, Dad says he's arranged for someone special to come and open the event, but he won't say who it is! He's being very secretive."

Neil went to the kitchen to get some cans of lemonade from the fridge. Through the kitchen window, he could see Tim. Only he wasn't playing football. To Neil's surprise, he and Jake were fooling around with Jake's rubber bone.

For the first time ever, Neil saw Tim laugh with pleasure.

Neil opened the kitchen door and casually wandered outside. As soon as Tim saw him, he stopped playing with Jake and assumed his usual moody expression. He swung a foot at the football, slamming it against the wall.

"Jake looked as if he was enjoying himself," said Neil. "And so did you. You didn't have to stop for me."

Jake barked and ran off a few paces, daring Tim to give chase. Tim turned away.

Neil understood how awful Tim must feel, moving to a new house, a new school, and losing his dog. It wasn't long ago that he'd had to cope with the pain of losing Sam. And he could imagine how jealous Tim must feel of Charlie. Not only was she always the centre of attention but now she had a new dog of her own.

"What was Cosmo like?" he asked gently. Tim just shook his head, and stepped away a few paces further.

"OK," said Neil, "but if you ever want to talk, I'd be happy to listen. And you can visit the dogs here any time."

Neil went back inside. "Now, about going on local radio," he said, handing round lemonade and biscuits to Emily and Charlie, "what do you think?"

"Surely it's not as simple as all that?" Charlie replied uncertainly.

"It won't be a problem," said Emily. "All you need to do is phone Tony Bradley from the 'Tell Tony' programme. He's an old friend of ours. Why don't you try him now? We've got the number here."

"I don't know," murmured Charlie. "I'm not sure I want to."

"He's really easy to talk to," said Neil, trying to be helpful. "You never know, you might be able to get him to come along on the day."

"Wouldn't that be great?" Emily enthused.

"Look . . . can I think about it?" Charlie hesitated.

"I don't see what the problem is," Neil said irritably. Why was Charlie being so difficult when they were all working their socks off?

Charlie got to her feet and pulled Chloe up with her. "There's a lot you don't understand, Neil. All right?" She spoke angrily. "You only wanted me to come with you to Richard Hammond's place to get his sympathy. And now you want me to do the same with the man at the radio station. Maybe I don't always want the most important thing about me to be that I'm blind. Now, can you ask your mum if she'll take us home. If not, we'll walk!"

Neil suddenly felt very small, and couldn't think of anything to say.

The next evening Neil and Emily came home from school to find a message on the answer machine.

"It's Charlie," the voice said. "I'm really sorry about yesterday. Sometimes it just all gets too much, you know. It can feel like I'm always walking on eggshells with Mum and Tim. Anyway, I've done it. I'm going to be on Tony Bradley's show tomorrow afternoon, and we'll plug the walk and the cause of guide dogs for all we're worth, won't we, Chloe?"

There was an answering woof in the background.

"So, if there's anything you want me to say, call me back. Otherwise, I'll come round tomorrow evening and we'll go to the Hammonds' farm. Bye!"

Neil breathed a sigh of relief.

Charlie was great on the radio. She sounded relaxed and confident as Tony teased from her the story of how she and Chloe had met. He asked Chloe jokingly if she had anything she wanted to say to the world and Chloe responded with a barked message of her own. Then Tony asked people to phone in with offers of sponsorship for Charlie and Chloe. He promised on air that he'd try his very best to be at The Grange for the start of the walk.

"Well done, Charlie," exclaimed Emily as they met outside Old Mill Farm later on that evening. "You were brilliant." Jake bounced up at her to add his congratulations.

"And we mustn't leave you out," said Neil, going down to ruffle Chloe's neck. "What a great team!" Chloe wagged her tail in delight.

"Now let's see how good we are at getting Richard Hammond on our side," said Charlie. "Come on. I don't expect you want to do this any more than I do."

Jane Hammond answered the door and showed them through into the living room where they all sank into the comfortable chairs and sofa. The Hammonds' dog Delilah was Jake's mother. She spotted Jake, and the two dogs greeted each other noisily, paws and noses locked in a friendly tussle, before settling down together by the fireplace. Chloe lay by Charlie's feet.

Richard Hammond was sitting reading a paper, which he'd put down as they came in. In contrast to Jane, who was small and neat, Richard's long thin legs stuck out in front of him untidily.

"This is all very mysterious," he said. "A deputation! What's it all about then?"

When they explained, Richard Hammond's ears went red and Jane left the room hurriedly. For a moment, Neil feared the worst.

Richard cleared his throat. "I see," he said nervously. "Yes, well, I'm afraid you've rather caught me out on that one. Jane's been telling me I ought to do something about it for months. I never meant to block the path, you know. It was the wretched builders not clearing up after themselves when we had a conversion done to the side of the house. Still, you don't want to know about that. I expect you want to know what I'm going to do about it."

They nodded their heads politely while Richard drank from a cup of tea. He seemed determined to keep them in suspense.

"Well. . ." He looked at Neil, Emily and Charlie. "I'll have all the rubbish moved by the weekend. And if there's anything more we can do to help the walk, we'll be delighted. I think it was very brave of you to come and see me."

As the day of the walk got closer there were a lot of jobs to do and people to see. Carole arranged for members of the local Women's Institute to man the stopping points. Bob made sure there'd be enough drinks available for walkers and their dogs. Neil, Emily and Charlie checked that all the walkers had a copy of the route. Most important of all, everybody was working hard on finding as much sponsorship as possible, right up to the last minute.

The evening before the walk, Neil found Bob hanging by his hands from the lintel of the barn door.

"What on earth are you up to, Dad? You'll do yourself an injury."

"I've *done* myself the injury, Neil. I'm trying to make it better now," said Bob. "This is supposed to be good for the back."

"It doesn't look it," replied Neil. Then he added, "Dad, I'm worried. Do you think it's going to be OK tomorrow? Will there be enough people there?"

Bob dropped down, wincing as his feet took

the weight of his body. "Well, it's too late to worry now, Neil. But I've got a hunch it might be a day to remember. You'll see."

"And there's one other thing," added Neil. "I'm dying to know who this mystery guest is you've got lined up."

Bob tapped his nose. "That's between me and this doorpost," he laughed. "But you'll find out soon enough, won't you?"

Chapter Six

y nine o'clock on Saturday morning, June the fourteenth, it was already hot in the courtyard of King Street Kennels, and it was getting hotter by the minute.

"We've provided enough water at the stopping points, haven't we? And they're all in the shade, aren't they?" Neil asked his dad, hopping from foot to foot. "I'm worried about the dogs in this heat."

"Neil, just relax," said Bob, smiling. "It's unlike you to be so wound up. From what I hear the Women's Institute are going to make sure there's enough food and drink to cater for an army, and the St John's ambulance people have agreed to be on hand too. It'll be fine.

Since we're not walking, your mum and I'll keep an eye on things. We'll keep in touch with each stopping point on the mobile."

"It's just so important that everything goes right," said Neil.

"Maybe next time we won't start the walk in the midday heat!" said Bob, laughing. "Mind you, next time it'll probably snow."

The doorbell rang.

"Go and answer it, then," prompted Bob.

Waiting on the doorstep were Max Hooper and Prince, Max's beautiful golden cocker spaniel. A taxi zoomed out of the drive on its way back to the station.

Max was the star of Neil and Emily's favourite TV programme, *The Time Travellers*. When an episode of the series had been made at Padsham Castle, Max and Neil had become friends, drawn together by their love of dogs.

"Max, what are *you* doing here?" exclaimed Neil. "It's brilliant to see you both, but you've chosen kind of a funny day to drop in."

Max looked at him strangely. "I know," he said.

"What do you mean, 'you know'?"

"Neil, you're being dense," Max laughed. "Why do you think I'm here?"

Light dawned. "*You're* the mystery guest who's going to declare us open, so to speak! That's great!" yelled Neil. "Come in. Come and see Jake, Prince!" But before Prince could nose his way past Neil, Jake came tumbling through the house, falling over his feet in excitement at seeing his old friend.

"Where's Princess?" asked Neil. Princess was Max's new puppy and Prince's daughter.

"I had to get here by train," said Max, "and I didn't think I could manage them both by myself. Princess is quite a handful now!"

*

At eleven o'clock everyone squeezed into the Range Rover for the short ride up to The Grange. Mrs Dickens and her residents had done a fantastic job. Bunting was strewn between the lamp-posts on the drive and right across the front of the imposing building. A starting line had been constructed between two posts, and half a dozen tables with parasols were scattered among the beech trees on the lawn. Already there were people and dogs waiting expectantly.

Syd was standing on the front steps talking to Charlie, Mr Bradshaw, and another old gentleman wearing a bright blue shirt who looked as if he might be Charlie's grandad. Syd caught sight of Neil and Emily and called, "Isn't this fantastic? What a brilliant day for it!"

Tony Bradley was wandering about with a tape recorder and a microphone, talking to anyone who looked interesting and desperately trying to avoid Mrs Jepson, King Street Kennels' least favourite customer. She was dressed in a shiny blue shellsuit and had tied matching ribbons on to her two spoilt Westies, Sugar and Spice. She was following the radio DJ every-where, obviously very keen for an interview, and her husband was shuffling after her looking rather embarrassed. As soon as Tony Bradley saw Max and Prince arrive, he made a swift beeline for them.

"Hey, there's Mrs Atkinson," said Emily. "Come on, Jasmine! Let's take you over to your partner for the day."

Jasmine picked herself up reluctantly and, already panting heavily, lumbered over to the old lady.

"Now, are you two going to be OK?" asked Neil anxiously. "You'll make sure you give Jasmine plenty to drink, won't you?"

"Oh yes, I'll make sure she's just fine, won't I, Jas?" said Mrs Atkinson, stooping down to stroke the Labrador fondly. "Don't you worry, Neil. Once your mother's taken us up to King Street we'll have a couple of hours together to get used to each other before we do any walking. We'll wait for Mr Brewster and Skip to arrive, and then we'll walk up to Padsham with them."

"That's good," said Neil to Emily as they left the pair to their own devices. "They ought to be safe with Jim."

Skip, Jim Brewster's Border collie, was Sam's brother. He looked so like Sam that every time Neil saw him, his heart missed a beat.

As the clock approached midday, Neil and

Emily watched more and more walkers assemble. Eventually Max and Prince climbed to the top step of The Grange's entrance. Max thanked everyone for agreeing to take part and introduced Syd. She said a few words about the Guide Dogs for the Blind Association and how important the money raised that day would be, before handing back to Max.

"Well, good luck everyone," he shouted. "Have a happy, safe walk. Are you on your marks? Then get set . . . and *go!*"

At various speeds the crowd made their way through the gate, round the corner, and off towards the footpath that would eventually lead them to King Street.

Neil and Emily had agreed that they and Jake would walk with Charlie and Chloe. Charlie's mum and Tim were walking too, with Kip, an affectionate mongrel that had arrived in the rescue centre a fortnight ago.

"It'll be really good for her," said Charlie to Neil and Emily. "Mum's bound to make some friends today. That's what she needs."

"Be careful, Charlie," said Mrs Elliott anxiously to her daughter as she and Tim set off. "I'm still not sure it's a good idea for you to do this walk."

"Don't fuss, Mum," muttered Charlie irritably. "It's a *very* good idea. Just try to enjoy it! Come on, let's go," she added to Neil and Emily.

"There's no need to rush," said Neil. "I'm sure we can walk faster than some of this lot over a whole afternoon. Anyway, despite what some people seem to think, it's not a race. Did you see the way Dr Harvey went off with Finn and Sandy? It was like they'd got a train to catch."

"We actually *have* got a train to catch," said Max as he appeared behind them with Prince. "Sorry it was such a quick visit. It's been great to see you. Put us down for a tenner if you complete the course."

"*If?*" snorted Neil. "You might as well give us the ten quid now!"

They left The Grange with the last group of stragglers and turned out into the road. A signpost pointed the way across a large field, and Neil saw a posh Jaguar draw up by the kerb a hundred metres or so further on. Two Westies with bows between their ears and an unmistakeable broad figure crammed into a bright blue shellsuit were piling into it hurriedly.

"Hey! Look over there!" whispered Neil.

"It's Mrs Jepson!" said Emily. "What's she doing?"

"Well, it looks as though she's had enough already," laughed Neil.

"Poor Sugar and Spice!" said Emily. "I'm sure they could do with the exercise."

"Well, just as long as she doesn't claim they walked all the way round. It's not very fair on the people who've sponsored her," said Neil.

"Or on the rest of us!" laughed Charlie.

The walk was like one big party strung out over a dozen miles. People chatted as they strolled along, and everyone was in high spirits. Most of the dogs were in a party mood too, bounding ahead of their owners, and chasing each other in circles in the empty open fields.

Neil, Charlie and Emily arrived at King Street just before one o'clock. It seemed like an open day with dogs everywhere, and walkers wandering round the house and grounds with drinks and sandwiches in their hands.

"Well done, Neil," said Mr Hamley, trying not to spill his lemonade as Dotty, his boisterous Dalmatian, tugged at her lead impatiently, pulling him round in circles. "What a splendid event. I hope you're going to write something about this for the school magazine."

As far as Neil could tell, the only person who wasn't in a great mood seemed to be Tim. His mum was talking to Jake Fielding from the *Compton News*, whose ponytail bobbed up and down as he listened and took notes. Tim stood apart from them, tapping his foot impatiently.

"At school last week, I asked Tim if he wanted to come and visit the rescue centre and help with the dogs," said Neil to Charlie.

"It's no use, Neil." Charlie shook her head. "Maybe he'll get over Cosmo in time. But at the moment no one can talk to him. I know it's hard, but you've just got to leave him be."

They set off again, this time heading for the path that took them up on to the ridgeway. Here there was no escape from the full force of the sun, and it was a relief to eventually drop down into the woodland surrounding Padsham Castle. Neil found it fascinating to walk with Charlie and Chloe and see the marvellous trust that had built between them, even in such a short time. Chloe seemed to really look after her human companion, giving Charlie the confidence to deal with the awkward obstacles she faced in the woods at Padsham. Neil learnt that if he did have to help, he should never *take* Charlie's arm to guide her over a fallen tree or

over a stream, but rather offer her the chance to slip her arm inside his.

At Padsham Castle, Neil spotted Syd in the crowds. She was busy chatting to as many of the walkers as she could, but she waved when she saw them and called over. "Isn't it going well? No real casualties yet, though I've heard a few complaints about blisters."

"Yes," said Emily. "I think I've got one myself. Ouch!"

Neil could see that a few walkers were beginning to feel the pace. He spotted Alex Harvey, flat out in the shade under a tree. The doctor's dogs seemed to be lasting better than him, and were licking his face, keen to set off again.

"Look at the difference between those two!" Neil said to Emily as they watched Jake and Chloe. "As soon as we arrive somewhere, Jake just can't wait to say hello to everybody, but Chloe always conserves her energy. You never see her rush around."

"Do you think it's the breed or the training?" asked Emily.

"Bit of both, I reckon. Some Labs can be really daft!" replied Neil.

They pushed on towards Colshaw and the stopping point at Netherfield Farm, the furthest point of the walk. They were back in open country again now, and Neil's legs were beginning to ache. Where the paths crossed fields of corn or oil-seed, or where there were sheep, Jake had to be reined in on his lead. Neil realized how hard the walk must be for Charlie.

"Are you OK?" he asked her.

Her head was down and she was concentrating hard. "Fine, thanks," she said in reply, flashing Neil a smile. "Getting a bit tired, though." Beside her, Chloe ploughed gamely on, panting loudly but apparently eager to tackle the rest of the walk.

Charlie was visibly relieved when they reached Netherfield Farm. But as soon as they had sat down in the cool courtyard in front of the farmhouse, Mr Hamley rushed up to Neil.

"Your mum just phoned here," he said. "She wants you to call her back straight away. The phone's just inside, in the kitchen."

"Why, has something happened?" Neil asked, looking puzzled.

"Mrs Atkinson and Jasmine have gone missing."

Chapter Seven

"So what's going on?" said Emily when Neil had spoken to Carole. "They can't have just disappeared!"

"Mum says Mrs Atkinson and Jasmine never arrived at Padsham Castle. Apparently it's a good two hours since they left King Street," replied Neil. "They should have been at the castle ages ago."

"What about Jim Brewster and Skip?" asked Emily. "I thought they were supposed to be keeping them company."

"Hang on," said Neil, catching sight of a familiar black-and-white shape on the far side of the courtyard. "There's Skip. Jim Brewster can't be far away."

"There he is," cried Emily as Jim strolled round the side of the farm building, balancing a cup of tea.

"So perhaps Mrs Atkinson's here, after all. Maybe your mum just didn't spot her and she decided to carry on walking," Charlie added hopefully.

"Hey, Jim!" said Neil, calling him over. "Are Mrs Atkinson and Jasmine with you?"

Skip's ears pricked up and his tail wagged when he saw Jake. The two dogs sniffed each other in a friendly greeting. Jim Brewster looked worried as he began to explain what had happened. Mrs Atkinson had found the climb up on to the ridgeway really tiring, and she'd started to worry that she and Jasmine were holding Jim and Skip back.

"I told her it wasn't a problem," explained Jim, "but she wouldn't have it. She said she'd walk back to the last stage and get a lift. In the end she went on at me so much, I gave in, and we walked on ahead. We knew we shouldn't have, didn't we, Skip?" Skip put his head on one side and whined his agreement. "I wonder what she's gone and done?"

"Well, they can't have wandered far," Emily said calmly. "We know they're somewhere between King Street and Padsham. We'll just have to go and look for them."

"I'll come with you if you like," said Jim. "I feel really bad about this."

Neil thought for a moment, and then said, "No, Jim. You keep going. Don't worry, we'll find her."

He pulled the ordnance survey map of the area from his rucksack. "They're not going to be in the open," he said. "They'd have been spotted by now. I guess they must have got lost somehow – maybe in the woods at the back of the castle, though with all those people around, I can't see how."

Emily peered over Neil's shoulder. "In which case, if we take that footpath just there—" she pointed at a line on the map, "we can take a short cut behind the castle and be searching the woods in half an hour. What do you think?"

"Good idea," agreed Neil. "I'll just go and call Mum to let her know, and then let's do it. Are you up for this, Charlie?"

Chloe was already on her feet, raring to go. "You bet!" Charlie answered straight away.

The path they'd seen on the map did not seem much like a short cut as they walked back to the woods above Padsham Castle. By the time they were close to the route the walk had taken, even Jake's head was drooping.

Chloe was brilliant. She never seemed to put a foot wrong, and never tired of watching out for Charlie.

"You're a star, Chloe," said Neil. "What would we do without you?"

Once they were in the woods, they began to call Mrs Atkinson's name, but there was no reply.

Eventually the path began to skirt a clearing. Suddenly Chloe lurched forward on the end of her harness.

"What is it, Chloe?" asked Charlie urgently. "What have you spotted?"

The Labrador pulled Charlie forward towards a narrow path that led across the clearing and into the trees beyond.

"I think Chloe's on to something," said Charlie. "Maybe she's picked up Jasmine's scent."

"Careful, Charlie," said Neil, moving quickly through the undergrowth to her side and allowing her to slip her arm through his. "It's really rough just here."

They made their way carefully across the clearing. As they approached the other side,

Chloe put down her nose and sniffed long and hard. Then, as she lifted her head, Jasmine casually wandered out from the trees to greet her, looking as if she didn't have a care in the world.

"Jasmine," said Neil, joyfully falling on her and giving her a cuddle. "Where have you been? Where's Mrs Atkinson?"

They shouted out Mrs Atkinson's name again. Jasmine wagged her tail, turned round, and ambled off again. With Jake now leading the way and Chloe pulling Charlie along, they followed her as quickly as they could.

The ground rose ahead of them. It was littered with stones and it was difficult walking, particularly for Charlie. Eventually they heard a weak voice. "Over here. Over here!" As they came up over the rise, there was Mrs Atkinson, lying on the ground, her back against a boulder.

Jake reached her first. He pushed his wet nose straight into Mrs Atkinson's face.

"Well done, Chloe! Brilliant stuff, Jasmine!" Neil shouted. "Come here, Jake, and give Mrs Atkinson a bit of space."

"Oh, I'm so glad to see you!" she sighed. "I'm really sorry to cause all this trouble.

"We're pretty glad to see you too," said Emily. "Are you all right?"

"I've hurt my ankle," grimaced Mrs Atkinson. "I was just beginning to think we were going to be here all night. Still, Jasmine would have been excellent company, wouldn't you, Jasmine? I'm sure we'd have lived to tell the tale!" Jasmine plodded up to her and swiped her face with her tongue.

"What made you come up here, Mrs Atkinson?" asked Neil, trying very hard not to show his exasperation.

"Wild strawberries, Neil. It's a splendid place to go looking for them," said Mrs Atkinson

weakly. "I used to come up here years ago. I thought I'd say thank you to Jim for walking with us by collecting some for him. We must just have gone further from the path than we intended, mustn't we, Jasmine?"

Jasmine licked her face again.

"It's lucky you had Jasmine with you," said Neil. "How are we going to get you home? It looks as if we'll need a stretcher."

"I feel very stupid," said Mrs Atkinson. "I should never have come all the way up here."

"Don't worry," said Charlie soothingly. "Chloe and I will stay here with you and Jasmine. Neil, why don't you and Emily go back to Padsham Castle for some help? It'll be quicker without us."

"OK," agreed Neil. "We'll be as fast as we can, Mrs Atkinson."

Forgetting their tired legs and sore feet, Neil and Emily half-ran, half-walked across the rough ground back to the main path, and then sprinted down to the castle, where Bob and Carole were waiting anxiously. With them were Jim Brewster and Skip, who had come back to help.

"Well, we've found her, Dad," said Neil, breathing heavily. "But I think we'll need to give the St John's Ambulance people a call. She's hurt her ankle. I think we can get quite close to where she is if we take the Range Rover along one of the forest roads."

The St John's Ambulance volunteers arrived quickly, and the Parkers plus Jim and Skip piled into the Range Rover and bounced up the stony track through the woods till they were near the clearing.

Neil led them quickly through to where Mrs Atkinson was waiting. Sitting patiently by her side were Jasmine, Chloe and Charlie, the two dogs alert and watchful. The volunteers gently examined Mrs Atkinson and eased her on to their stretcher. Jim rushed to help and said, "I don't know what came over me, Mrs A. I knew it wasn't a good idea to leave you."

"No, no, it's my fault, Jim," she replied. "You mustn't blame yourself."

As they carefully picked their way back to the car, Jasmine walked faithfully beside the stretcher, always to Mrs Atkinson's left, even when the ground was at its roughest.

"I think we're going to have to take you for an X-ray, Mrs Atkinson," sighed the St John's team leader. "That ankle might be broken. Is there someone who can come with you? And who's going to look after your dog?"

"I'll go to the hospital with her," said Jim Brewster.

"And we'll look after Jasmine," said Emily. "Don't worry about that! She'll be a pleasure, won't you, girl?"

"Jasmine's just on loan, you see," Mrs Atkinson explained. "She's not *my* dog at all really."

"Not yet, she isn't," chuckled Neil, under his breath.

As they waved Mrs Atkinson, Jim and Skip goodbye from Padsham Castle, Neil checked his watch. It was five o'clock. He groaned. "Look at the time," he exclaimed. "Everyone else will be finishing the walk about now. Our day's been completely ruined. All that sponsorship up in smoke! What are we going to do now?"

Chapter Eight

There was no one left at Padsham Castle except Charlie and the Parkers. Maggie Jones the caretaker was on her rounds picking up a few remaining pieces of litter. Jake went over to say hello to her, while Chloe and Jasmine settled down on the shady side of the Range Rover.

"Well," said Bob thoughtfully, "I suppose we *could* give the three of you a lift back to Netherfield, and you could try to complete the walk tonight. . ."

Charlie spoke. "I don't know about the others, but I think I'd duck out of that. Sorry, but I've had enough for one day. And I think maybe Chloe has too."

Emily nodded her head in agreement. Neil pulled a disappointed face, still reluctant to give in.

"Wouldn't it be more sensible to complete the walk tomorrow, Neil?" asked Bob. "I'm sure everyone would understand, in view of what's happened?"

Neil frowned, but inside he knew what his dad was saying made sense. "OK," he said. "I don't like it, but you're right."

Once they were back at The Grange, Neil, Emily and Charlie quickly found themselves telling the tale of Mrs Atkinson's rescue to a small crowd of people over a welcome glass of cold orange juice. Syd was there, with Charlie's mum and Tim, and assorted residents, including Henry Bradshaw and Skye. There hadn't been so much excitement at The Grange in a long while. Chloe was grateful to be out of her harness at last, and was enjoying a romp with Jake under the trees. Jasmine took the chance for a well-earned nap by the conservatory, in a cool spot that was clearly a favourite of hers.

"It was Chloe who tracked down Mrs Atkinson. We just followed," Neil explained.

"You should have seen her and Charlie set off across the forest!"

From the corner of his eye, Neil saw Tim's lip curl into a sneer. Tim broke off from the group, narrowing a look of pure jealousy in his sister's direction. His mum seemed to ignore him.

All the time, more walkers were arriving with their dogs. Mr Hamley looked completely exhausted, though Dotty seemed to have the energy to go round a second time. The Jepsons were there and seemed suspiciously sprightly. Mr Jepson looked around nervously and fiddled with his cravat in an embarrassed way. Mrs

Jepson's bright blue shellsuit still looked immaculate, as did Sugar and Spice.

"Look, there's not a hair out of place!" whispered Emily. "No one's going to believe they've done the walk!"

Syd went to the top of the steps and cleared her throat. Someone banged a mug on a table for silence, and they all listened as Syd made a short speech thanking the walkers for their efforts. She told everyone how important fund-raising events were for the Association, and how impressed she was by Neil, Emily and Charlie. Finally she explained how Jasmine had been the real inspiration for the event, and asked everyone to keep a minute's silence in memory of Willy Mannion.

Afterwards they fell into twos and threes, tidying up and chatting. Syd and Charlie sat down in the evening sun at the foot of the steps.

As he carried a tray of glasses past them into the house, Neil heard Charlie suddenly ask Syd in a panicky voice, "Where's Chloe?"

He turned round and cast an eye over the lawns of The Grange. Jake had joined Jasmine, flat out by the conservatory, but Chloe was nowhere to be seen.

"That's very odd," Neil said to Syd and

Charlie. "Come to think of it, I've not seen her for a while."

"Perhaps Chloe's with your mum?" Syd offered. "I heard her say she was going up with your grandad to his room."

"Doubt it," said Charlie. "Neil, I'm worried. I can't believe that Chloe would just wander off, but can you have a quick look for her all the same? It was stupid of me to let her off the harness. I thought she'd be safe here, but if she wanders out into Compton, goodness knows what might happen."

Neil raced down towards the gates of The Grange. On his way he bumped into Emily and told her what had happened. She joined him, and Jake ran over to meet them at the gates, ears pricked. They looked both ways down the road outside and waited for a moment, hoping that a familiar doggy figure would bound out from behind a tree, or appear from round the bend in the road, but there was no sign of Chloe. The hot day had turned into a humid, sultry evening. Dark threatening clouds were beginning to roll in from the west. Outside The Grange, there was no one about.

They turned back and began to search round the edge of the grounds. But no Labrador came scrabbling from the shrubbery or running guiltily from the bottom of the vegetable garden.

"She's not here," said Emily.

"I know," answered Neil.

They went back to where Charlie and Syd were waiting by the steps.

"She's not with Mum either," said Charlie. "Syd went and asked. I didn't think she would be."

At that moment Mrs Elliott appeared at the top of the steps. "Have you found that nuisance of a dog?" she asked. Charlie shook her head miserably.

"I knew this would happen," said Mrs Elliott. She sounded so furious that Neil was quite shocked. "This is proof that the dog's plain unreliable," she continued. "I never thought it would work out. Let's just suppose, Charlotte, that this is October and you're by yourself in Oxford. What would happen to you?"

"I expect my friends would help me," said Charlie through gritted teeth. "Like Neil, Emily and Syd are doing now."

"Your *family* would be quite willing to help you," said her mum crossly, "if only you'd let them!"

"I'm sixteen, Mum," snapped Charlie. "I'm

sorry, but I don't always want to be with my family. I want to do other things with my life too."

Her mother's voice softened, "You're *only* sixteen, darling. I worry constantly that something dreadful will happen to you. Can't you see that?"

By now, Charlie really wasn't listening. "Let's face it, Mum," she said resentfully, "you don't want me to grow up. Has it occurred to you that you want me around for yourself, so that *you're* not lonely, and *you* don't have to try to make new friends?"

Neil and Emily studied the floor, embarrassed by this family row. Jasmine, hearing the sudden noise, woke up and strolled over, curious to see what was going on.

"Don't you see," said Mrs Elliott, sounding close to tears herself, "that Chloe just isn't ready to be left with someone like you? I'm sorry to have to say this, but clearly she can't have been trained properly. What with all that sickness—"

"Once!" interrupted Charlie. "And it was nothing—"

"What with all that sickness," her mum continued stubbornly, "she hasn't been right from the very beginning. Even if we do find her again I'm afraid she'll have to go back to Bolton."

Syd intervened gently. "I don't think that's quite fair, Mrs Elliott." She spoke softly. "Until we know what's really happened to Chloe, we shouldn't jump to any hasty conclusions. Obviously I'm a bit anxious myself, because if there *have* been any problems with Chloe's training, I'd feel partially responsible. But standing here arguing isn't going to help us find Chloe, is it?"

The firm, calm way Syd spoke took the heat out of the situation.

"You're quite right, Syd," said Mrs Elliott, looking embarrassed. "I'm sorry. I really shouldn't have spoken like that about your work. It was uncalled for. Come on, let's have another look for Chloe. Tim can help too."

"Where is Tim?" said Neil.

"Wasn't he with you? Don't you know where he is?" Mrs Elliott asked Charlie.

"If he won't talk to me, how am I supposed to know where he is all the time?" Charlie's words had a bitter edge to them.

Neil thought quickly. He remembered the sneering glances Tim had shot at his sister when they'd come back from finding Mrs

Atkinson. Tim was so jealous of Charlie and the attention he felt she was always getting, it wouldn't be at all surprising if he'd tried to get back at her by some means. And what more hurtful way could there be than through Chloe?

"I don't suppose Chloe could be with Tim?" Neil aimed his words at Mrs Elliott. "Do you think he might have taken her off somewhere? I mean, he doesn't always seem very happy, does he? I saw him playing with Jake the other day, and I think he misses having a dog terribly."

"I'm sure Tim would never harm Chloe," she said defensively.

"*I'm* not," muttered Charlie.

"No, Charlie," said Neil. "Your mum's right. He might be upset, but I'm sure he wouldn't do anything unkind."

"He's pretty unkind to me from time to time," was Charlie's sharp retort.

Bob and Carole Parker wandered over to the little group. Behind them trailed a weary-looking Sarah. With most of the walkers and their dogs on their way home, Carole had been helping Mrs Dickens put away the tables and chairs and take down the bunting. Bob had Kip with him, the mongrel King Street had loaned

Tim and Sylvia Elliott for the walk. He was leading him by the collar.

Neil and Charlie explained the situation. Bob looked serious.

"Well," he said, "maybe that explains why I found poor Kip roaming around without a lead."

"You think Tim might have borrowed it for Chloe?" said Neil. "It certainly makes sense. I don't see how he'd persuade her to go with him otherwise."

"Right," said Bob, "it's eight o'clock now, and from the look of the sky, there's every chance of a storm. We might only have an hour or so of light left. How long have Tim and Chloe been gone?"

"Half an hour at the outside," replied Neil.

"Normally I'd say we ought to give them some time to see if they come back of their own accord," Bob thought out loud. "But I suppose I'm right in thinking Tim doesn't know this area very well, am I, Sylvia?"

Sylvia Elliott nodded.

"Well then, I think we ought to give Sergeant Moorhead a ring straight away so that the police can keep a look out," Bob continued. "And perhaps we should think about splitting up and searching for them ourselves."

Sylvia Elliott rang Sergeant Moorehead from Bob's mobile. After a quick conversation she turned back to the group. "He'll be here shortly," she said.

"Good," said Neil. "I think we should do as you said, Dad, and start searching now." Half an hour ago he'd felt really tired, but with the urgency of the situation, that was all forgotten. "Why don't Charlie, Emily and I take Jake with us to search the route we walked this morning, up towards the ridgeway?" At the mention of his name, Jake stood to attention, tail wagging frantically. "And perhaps the rest of you could try the paths up behind The Grange? Will your back be OK, Dad?" Neil added.

"It's stood up to today pretty well, actually. I'll be fine," Bob assured him, looking across at Mrs Elliott. "I'm just a bit concerned about you three going off on your own."

"We know those paths better than anyone, because we use them so often for walking the dogs," said Neil confidently. "Once we're over the stile, the walking's easy enough. If Charlie keeps hold of one of us, she'll be fine." Charlie nodded her head vigorously.

Mrs Elliott opened her mouth to protest, and then, seeing her daughter's stubborn look, thought twice about it and kept quiet.

"Why don't I give Neil my mobile?" said Syd. "That way, we can all keep in touch. And I can't go off searching on my own anyway. I haven't a clue where I am!"

Mrs Dickens had been standing behind them listening to their plans.

"How about leaving Sarah with me?" she asked. "Come on up to my room, love, and I'll read you a story."

"About hamsters?" asked a sleepy Sarah.

"Of course," answered Mrs Dickens. "If that's what you'd like!"

At that moment Jasmine picked herself up from her spot by the conservatory and, perhaps as she always used to do, walked straight through the middle of them, into The Grange and up the stairs, looking for Willy Mannion's room and her basket.

"Jasmine will be all right here too," said the matron. "We'll make sure she's comfortable. You'd better go before it gets dark! Don't forget to take a torch with you."

And with the skies darkening by the minute, they hurried off their separate ways to look for Tim and the missing guide dog.

Chapter Nine

The bars of the stile showed black against the indigo-blue of the evening sky as Neil, Emily, Charlie and Jake turned off the road outside The Grange to begin the route of the sponsored walk for the second time that day.

"Ever got the feeling you've been somewhere before?" joked Charlie.

"Do you think we can get anyone to cough up for the second time around as well?" said Neil. Suddenly serious again, he looked at Charlie and asked, "Are you sure you're all right doing this?"

"You don't get it, do you, Neil?" replied Charlie angrily. "Chloe's my dog and Tim's my brother. I'm hardly likely to want to leave it to everyone else, am I?"

Jake gave a whine of distress at Charlie's sharp voice, and nuzzled her hand. She stroked his head to comfort him.

"OK, OK!" said Neil defensively. "Point taken. I just didn't want you to do something you were unhappy with. Here we go, then."

They set out along the track. The light was getting dimmer by the minute and the detail of the bushes faded into dark blurry shapes.

"It must be getting dark now. Hope you've all been eating your carrots!" said Charlie, trying to lighten the mood after her outburst. There was a moment's pause and then she added sincerely, "I've been meaning to say to you guys, I really appreciate everything you've tried to do for our family, and for the Association. However this turns out, you've both been fantastic. I won't forget it, I promise you."

"No problem," said Neil, embarrassed by the sudden compliment. "It's all been loads of fun – well, until now."

On their left the fields fell away towards the river, which in the fading light was becoming a black gash across the landscape. On their right the dark outline of a clump of woodland hung above them. As they reached its edge, there was a loud crash from the branches of the trees. All three of them jumped.

"What's that?" cried Charlie.

A bird with a huge wingspan slowly flapped its way out over the fields to begin its evening hunt.

"It's only a barn owl," sighed Emily in relief.

They walked on a couple of hundred metres, with Jake in front of them, rooting through the grass at the side of the track. Suddenly he stopped dead, ears pricked.

"What is it, Jake? What have you heard?" asked Neil, bending down and touching Jake's collar with his hand. Jake growled, shot a look at Neil over his shoulder, and bounded off into the undergrowth on the right.

"Stay here, you two. I'll follow him," shouted Neil, and he dived after Jake into the woodland. Even twenty metres from the track, Neil realized that he had no chance of keeping up with the young Border collie. The beam of the torch his dad had given him only carried a few metres in the dense thicket, and he was so unsure of his footing that it became impossible for him to go any further.

"Jake," he shouted. "Jake, come back!"

Hoping that his dog had caught wind of Tim and Chloe, he tried calling for them too, but there was no answer. All he heard was a crashing in the vegetation that could have been another person, or Jake, or a deer for that matter.

"What's going on?" called Charlie from behind him.

"Don't know," he yelled back. "Hang on!"

He waited and waited in the gloom. He was just beginning to think that he'd have to turn back, when Jake bounced into the pencil of light from the torch and shot past him back to where Charlie and Emily stood.

"Oh, Jake, we don't need this," moaned Neil in exasperation as he dragged himself out of the brambles. "This is no time for a game!"

"Whatever it was, I don't think it was Tim and Chloe," said Emily.

"Rabbits probably," said Neil gloomily. "We're running out of time here. Look at that sky."

Overhead, Neil and Emily could see an evil-looking mass of cloud that threatened to block out the rising moon. From the distance came a rumble of thunder. Jake gave a low growl.

They ploughed on up the track. They walked in silence now, and every crack of a twig, every scrape of their feet on the hard earth of the track sounded deafening.

Suddenly Charlie pulled on Neil's arm. "What's that?" she said breathlessly.

"Not you too," said Neil. "I didn't hear anything."

"Maybe *you* didn't." Charlie replied sharply. "Just listen. *Really* listen, will you?"

They strained their ears, but no sound came back to Emily and Neil from the country around them.

Then Charlie gave another start. "There it is again," she cried. "It's a bark! From down there!" She gestured towards the river.

"I really couldn't hear anything," said Neil. "Are you sure?"

"Trust me," said Charlie. "I've got great hearing. Remember, I've always had to concentrate on sounds because they're all I've got. Is there a way down to the left?"

Neil and Emily peered down the track. They could just make out the suggestion of a path leading over the field.

"Could be," said Neil. "Let's give it a try."

They picked their way along the curving track as it snaked between hedges and through the corners of fields, past the dark shapes of old farm machinery. Charlie stopped again. "Now can you hear?"

"You're right," said Emily. "It's definitely a bark."

"And it's definitely Chloe," said Charlie. "Quick, Neil, let's keep going. I just hope they're both OK."

Neil could hear the sound of the water now, and ahead of them he could see the shapes of stone buildings. Then, suddenly, the barking became clearer and there was Chloe, bounding out of one of the buildings and up the track to greet them.

Chloe had eyes only for Charlie. Bottom

wiggling with excitement and joy, Chloe clambered all over Charlie's crouched figure, licking her face, while Charlie, almost crying with relief, made a huge fuss of the now rather dirty Labrador.

"Where on earth have you been, you naughty girl?" she said. "And where's Tim?"

Chloe barked loudly and took a few steps towards the buildings, her tail wagging frantically. Jake went to join her.

"He must be down there." Neil seized Charlie's arm. "It looks like there are some old ruins by the river. I'm sure I remember Mr Bradshaw telling me there was an old watermill down here. Maybe that's where Chloe's taking us. She seems to know where she's going. Go, Chloe! Show us where Tim is! Good dog!"

The two dogs needed little encouragement, and ran down to the buildings ahead of them.

Neil, Emily and Charlie followed and, as they came near the old watermill, they began to hear Tim's muffled voice calling out desperately from inside, matched by a chorus of barks from Chloe.

"Tim, are you OK?" shouted Charlie anxiously.

Even in the dim light, Neil could see the

building was in a poor state. The outer part had no roof, and where the front door should have been there was only a pile of rubble.

He shone his torch into the darkness. It lit up a doorway leading to a second room. "Let me follow Chloe inside on my own," he said. "It's too difficult for all of us with only the one torch. We don't want anyone else getting hurt today." Charlie and Emily reluctantly agreed.

Carefully, Neil clambered over the rubble and went through the second doorway. "Tim?" he called softly.

"I'm over here," answered a shaking, frightened voice, only just audible above the roar of the river water.

It took a while for Neil's eyes to acclimatize to the dark, even with the torch. There were gaping holes in the mill roof, through which the sky could be seen, and old rotting timbers lay piled up in one corner. Part of the river ran right through the mill, just centimetres from Chloe's feet, and the slot where the waterwheel and its paddles had once fitted was clearly visible. Sitting on top of a stone platform on the other side of the water was a miserable-looking Tim. He was drawn up into himself, hugging his knees. The remains of a makeshift wooden bridge trailed down into the stream in front of him. There was a drop of maybe three metres into its churning flow.

"The wood broke," Tim said in a trembling voice. "It's too far to jump back. I thought no one would ever find us."

"Don't panic," said Neil, joining Chloe on the edge. "If you could get a run at the stream, you might be OK, but it's too tricky from a standing start. Give me a few seconds."

"What's going on?" shouted Charlie from behind him.

"Tim's OK," Neil reassured her, "but we've got a bit of a problem to sort out."

"I'll phone Dad and let them know we've found him," Emily said.

"Let's see what this wood is like," Neil shouted over to Tim, positioning the torch so that it pointed at the wood stacked in the corner. He hauled on a couple of the timbers and tested them with his foot. They split and crumbled immediately.

"Don't fancy those!" he muttered to himself. He pulled out more planks, testing them one by one until eventually he found two that seemed sound.

"As I push these over, grab them," he

shouted to Tim. "They'll take your weight."

Shakily, Tim got to his feet and looked down at the drop to the water below. In the torchlight, Neil saw that Tim's face was white and scared. "It'll be OK. If it was an ordinary path, you wouldn't think twice about it," encouraged Neil.

Tim put a foot on to the planks and then withdrew it. "I can't," he said.

"Of course you can," said Neil more firmly. "Just look at me. Come on!"

In the doorway, Emily crouched by Jake and held her breath.

"Tell me what's happening," cried Charlie desperately.

"It'll be all right. Really it will," Emily said, then quickly explained what was going on.

Suddenly Chloe brushed past Neil and darted nimbly across the planks to Tim. She nudged him gently with her nose then quickly turned round and walked back across the makeshift bridge to Neil.

"Look! Chloe's showing you the way," said Neil. "If she can do it, so can you. Well done, girl," he added to Chloe, bending down to ruffle the Labrador's fur.

This was all the encouragement that Tim needed. Slowly he inched his way on to the wood and, with arms stretched wide like a high-wire act, balanced his way across. In the middle he teetered and bent double, and for a heart-stopping moment Neil thought he would fall into the water, but he recovered and ran the last couple of metres. Behind him one of the planks, loosened by the vibration, banged down into the stream.

"He's made it!" cried Emily.

Charlie breathed again.

Tim clung to Chloe in sheer relief at having made it.

"Well done, Tim! Great stuff, Chloe!" said Neil. *What more does Chloe have to do to convince Mrs Elliott she's made of the right stuff?* he thought.

Chapter Ten

Outside the watermill, Neil and Emily watched as Charlie slipped Chloe back into her harness, talking softly to her and stroking her back. Tim stood beside her, looking small and wretched. Charlie just frowned at him, for once lost for words.

They trudged back towards The Grange in a horrible silence. As Neil's torch picked out the bends of the track, Jake walked quietly beside him, apparently subdued.

Halfway to the road, a more powerful beam of light swung down the path towards them. It was Bob and Syd, with Sergeant Moorhead. There was relief in their voices as they saw that neither Chloe or Tim were injured.

When they reached The Grange, Sylvia Elliott rushed up the drive to meet them, wrapping Tim in a hug. "Thank goodness you're safe," she breathed. Then she took him by the shoulders and, looking him straight in the eyes, asked, "What were you thinking about, Tim? We were *so* worried."

Tim explained haltingly that he hadn't meant to scare anyone or hurt Chloe. In fact she'd come with him willingly enough, once he'd clipped on Kip's lead.

A few months previously, when he'd been visiting his grandad at The Grange, they'd got chatting with old Willy Mannion. They'd been

talking about local walks, and the old man had mentioned that when he wanted to think, he and Jasmine used to stroll down to the watermill and sit by the river.

"Willy played there when he was our age," said Tim. "When the watermill was still working." He stopped and gulped. "I needed to think too, so I decided to take Chloe down there to have a look. Or rather, she took me. She almost seemed to know the way. But then I was stupid," he continued. "I knew it wasn't safe to try to get across to the other side of the stream. The wooden bridge broke, and I was stuck. I tried to get Chloe to go and find help, but she wouldn't leave me until the others turned up."

When he'd finished, there was a pause. Neil felt a large raindrop hit him on the nose, and Jake gave a bark as the wind suddenly picked up.

Charlie broke the silence. "Can we go home now?" she asked in a small, cold voice.

"I think we'd all be better off at home," said Sergeant Moorhead. "Looks like that storm's finally about to break."

Late the next morning, after a much-needed lie-in, Neil and Emily walked Jake and Jasmine up to Railway Cottages to see how Mrs Atkinson was.

"I'm so stiff today," said Emily as they set off.

"Me too," agreed Neil. "Dad's the only one who's not suffering. His back seems to be completely cured! To be honest, I'm not really looking forward to finishing the walk today!"

They found Mrs Atkinson sitting on a cushion in the front garden of Railway Cottages with a heavily-strapped ankle stretched out in front of her. With some difficulty she was pulling weeds from a flower bed and dropping them into a barrow. Jasmine stepped delicately over the old woman's legs and pushed her face affectionately into Mrs Atkinson's.

"Come to help with the gardening, have you, Jasmine?" said Mrs Atkinson patiently, reaching up to stroke the Labrador's neck. "Aren't you a love?"

"How did it go at the hospital last night?" asked Neil.

"Well, it was a long wait," said Mrs Atkinson, "but the good news is there's nothing broken. Just a really bad sprain."

Jasmine wandered off round the garden, and then in through the open front door of Railway Cottages.

"Hey, Jas, come out of there!" shouted Emily.

"Let her be. She's all right," said Mrs Atkinson. "It's nice to see she feels at home. She was wonderful company on the walk. I shall miss her not being around today."

"Well," said Neil slowly, "that's really what we've come about, apart from finding out how you are. We wondered whether you might like Jasmine to stay with you?"

"Have a holiday here, you mean? To help you out? I don't know how you Parkers manage with so many dogs to look after."

"If you like," said Neil, smiling. "But if you still get on well in a week or so, perhaps you'd want to keep her. We'd need to tell the Guide Dogs for the Blind Association where she's living, and they'd probably come and visit you to see that Jas is OK, but I'm sure they'd be pleased when they saw what a good home she had."

Mrs Atkinson's face lit up. Jasmine walked back out of the house, and placed one paw carefully on Mrs Atkinson's good leg.

"I think that's a magnificent idea. What kind people you are!" she said. "She'll be welcome company after all this time. I've really missed having a dog, you know."

Jasmine gave a short bark of approval, and licked her hand.

After lunch Carole gave Neil and Emily a lift to see Charlie. Bob had worked out that, if all the walkers managed to collect their sponsorship money, they would have raised about two thousand pounds. Neil couldn't wait to tell Charlie the good news.

The Elliotts' house was a converted barn set back from the Colshaw road, looking out over a field of blue flax. When Neil, Emily and Jake arrived everyone was sitting on the patio. Charlie and Syd were talking in low voices, Tim was reading, and Mrs Elliott gave the impression of being unable to settle to anything. One moment she was wandering off into the kitchen and moving dishes around. Then she was pacing up and down in the garden looking anxiously at Tim and Charlie. As Neil and Emily arrived she drew them to one side.

"I'm really sorry about Tim's behaviour, you two," she said, looking embarrassed. "I told him he ought to call you to thank you for all you've done."

Neil and Emily didn't know what to say. Neil mumbled that it had been nothing really, and he and Emily quickly went over to join Charlie and Syd. Emily sat by Chloe on the grass. As she ran her fingers through the Labrador's short sleek hair, Chloe rolled over to have her tummy tickled.

Charlie seemed subdued, although she cheered up a bit when Neil told her how much they'd raised for the Guide Dogs for the Blind Association. Syd was really excited.

"That's fantastic. It will help a lot towards the advanced training of a guide dog," she said. "It's almost as if you – and everyone who took part – helped pay for Charlie to have Chloe."

"That's ace!" said Emily. "We get a framed photograph of a guide dog to keep too. We'll have to have Chloe in the picture."

Chloe wagged her tail as Charlie stroked her absent-mindedly.

"How's things?" Neil asked Charlie.

"Not great!" she whispered, glancing in her brother's direction. "I don't feel quite as angry with him as I did. But he doesn't seem a bit grateful that we dug him out of a hole. And Mum's being really uptight 'cos she's so worried about him."

Syd nodded her head sympathetically.

"I can't believe it," added Charlie. "What's it going to take to convince him that life's not quite so bad?"

Neil wasn't sure whether Tim had heard his sister, but suddenly he flung his book on to the patio and shouted, "Why are you all looking at me? Why are you talking about me behind my back? I've had enough! I can't stand being with any of you any more." Fighting back angry tears, he ran into the house. They heard the sound of doors slamming and then, through the passageway beside the cottage, Neil saw Tim setting off down the road in the direction of Colshaw. Neil acted decisively.

"Come on, Jake," he said. "Here we go again. Let's go and get Tim."

"It won't do any good," warned Charlie as Neil headed off.

Tim hadn't gone very far. It was almost as if he hoped somebody would come after him. Neil found him a few hundred metres down the road, hanging over a field gate.

Neil felt angry at the other boy's rudeness and ungratefulness. "Look, I can understand you're upset, but don't you think you should give Charlie and your mum a chance," he said quietly as he and Jake came level with Tim.

Tim turned and faced him.

"You don't know what it's like." He scowled. "No one does!"

"What don't I know?" asked Neil. "What it's like to lose a dog I loved? But I *do* know – I really do." And he told Tim about Sam, Jake's father, who'd died so recently. When he'd finished, there was a silence. The wind rustled the trees and grass. Tim looked crestfallen, and Jake whined and put his paws up on Tim's legs.

"No one'll ever replace Cosmo," said Neil. "Just like Jake here could never be the same as Sam. But there's always something new – you've just got to look for it. Spend time with us at King Street. Perhaps you could even become a puppy-walker for the Guide Dog Association. And maybe one day Cosmo will be able to come back. It's not hopeless, is it?"

"I suppose not," Tim admitted reluctantly.

"I know it's hard but I reckon you've got to make it up with Charlie," Neil said.

Tim nodded and they began to walk slowly back towards the Elliotts' house. As they reached the gate, Neil asked, "How d'you feel? D'you think you can face everyone now?"

Tim swallowed hard. "Yes," he said. "I think so."

Sylvia Elliott was waiting for them anxiously. Tim gave his mum a hug and then, as Chloe padded over to add her welcome, he walked up to his sister and said, "I'm really sorry, Charlie."

As Neil, Emily and Jake prepared to leave half an hour later, the Elliott household was a much happier one.

"I must say a thank you to you two," said Mrs Elliott. "You've both been really good friends to Charlie and Tim. Thanks to you, and to your sponsored walk, we all feel much happier about being in Compton. I've always thought I'll feel terribly lonely when Charlie goes to Oxford, but now . . . well, it doesn't seem so bad after all. Now I know Tim and I've got friends we can rely on!"

Syd's cheery face appeared at Mrs Elliott's shoulder. "Compton's great, isn't it?" She smiled. "Just tell your dad, Neil, that if ever he needs another helping hand at King Street Kennels, he ought to give me a ring. Maybe it's time I moved on from Bolton."

Neil grinned back. "You want to watch out, Syd. We just might take you up on that!"

Charlie appeared from the house with Chloe in her harness.

"We need a lift up the road, Mum," she said.

Neil and Emily looked puzzled.

"Well, we've got a walk to finish, haven't we?" Charlie smiled.

From behind them, they suddenly heard Tim's voice. "Can I come too?" he asked.

Charlie turned round, surprised, and Chloe pulled forward and gave Tim's hand an affectionate lick. "Yeah," Charlie said, smiling. "Of course you can. Two's good company but six is a lot more fun!"

PUPPY PATROL titles available from
Macmillan Children's Books

The prices shown below are correct at the time of going to press. However, Macmillan Publishers reserve the right to show new retail prices on covers which may differ from those previously advertised.

JENNY DALE

All Macmillan titles can be ordered at your local bookshop or are available by post from:

Book Service by Post
PO Box 29, Douglas, Isle of Man IM99 1BQ

Credit cards accepted. For details:
Telephone: 01624 675137
Fax: 01624 670923
E-mail: bookshop@enterprise.net

Free postage and packing in the UK.
Overseas customers: add £1 per book (paperback)
and £3 per book (hardback).